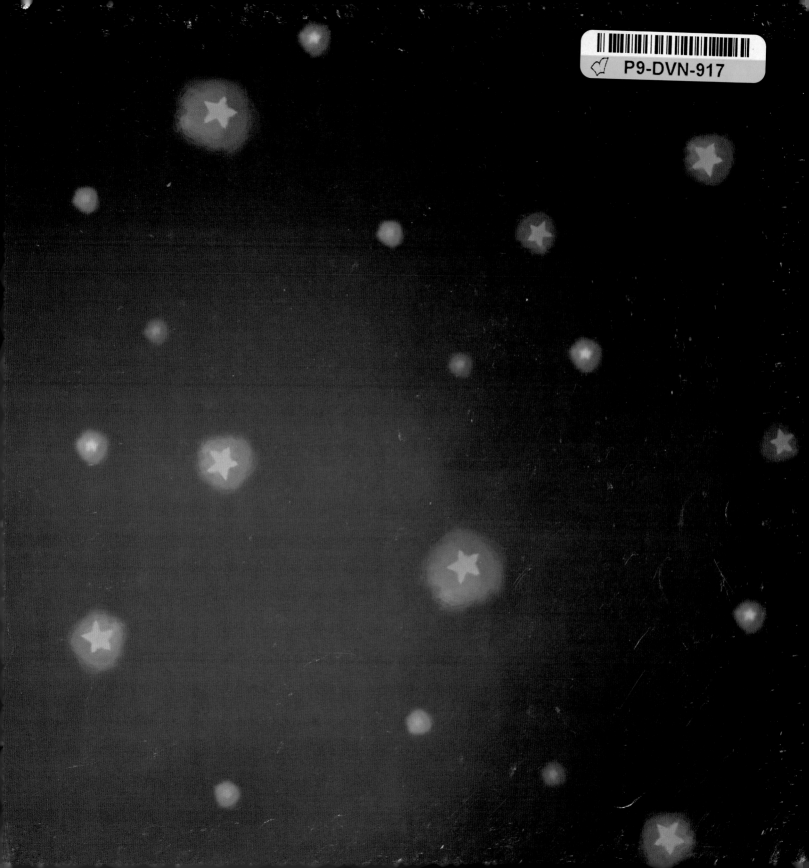

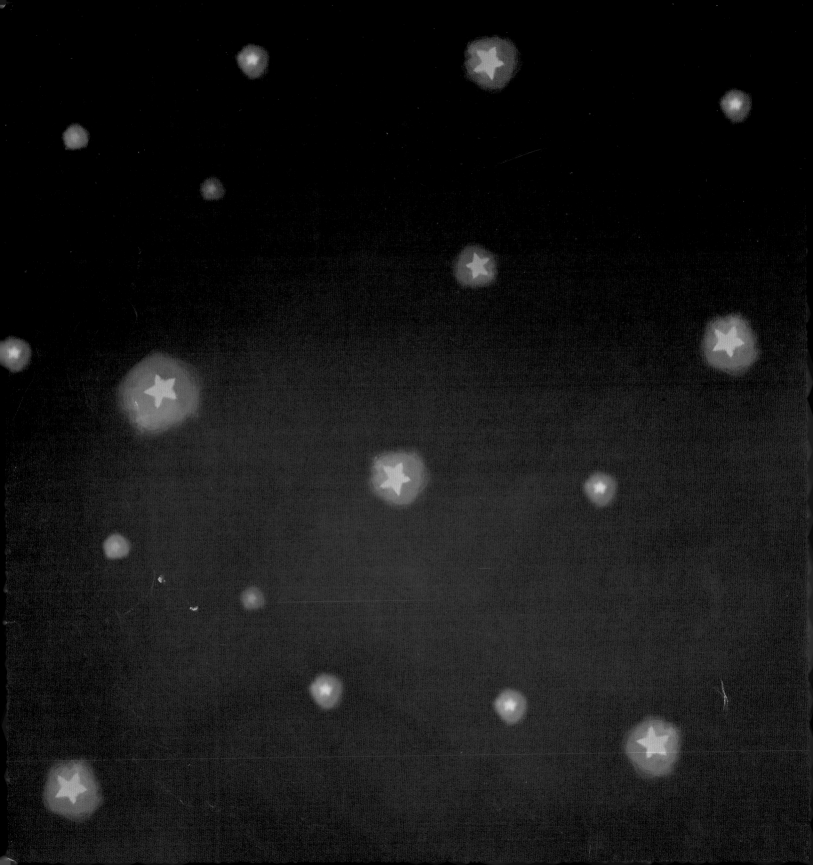

This book belongs to

**STERLING CHILDREN'S BOOKS**
New York

An Imprint of Sterling Publishing
387 Park Avenue South
New York, NY 10016

ISBN 978-1-4027-9070-6 (hardcover)

Library of Congress Cataloging-in-Publication Data
Selig, Josh.
  Red & Yellow's noisy night / by Josh Selig ; illustrations by Little Airplane Productions.
    p. cm.
  ISBN 978-1-4027-9070-6
  I. Little Airplane Productions. II. Olive branch (Television program) III. Title. IV. Title: Red
and Yellow's noisy night.
  PZ7.S4569256Re 2013
  [E]--dc23

                                        2011033448

Distributed in Canada by Sterling Publishing
C/o Canadian Manda Group, 165 Dufferin Street
Toronto, Ontario, Canada M6K 3H6

For information about custom editions, special sales, and premium and corporate purchases,
please contact Sterling Special Sales at 800-805-5489 or specialsales@sterlingpublishing.com.

Designed by Merideth Harte

Printed in China
Lot #:
2  4  6  8  10  9  7  5  3  1
11/11

www.sterlingpublishing.com/kids

THE OLIVE BRANCH

# Red & Yellow's
# Noisy Night

## by Josh Selig

illustrations by
Little Airplane Productions

STERLING CHILDREN'S BOOKS
New York

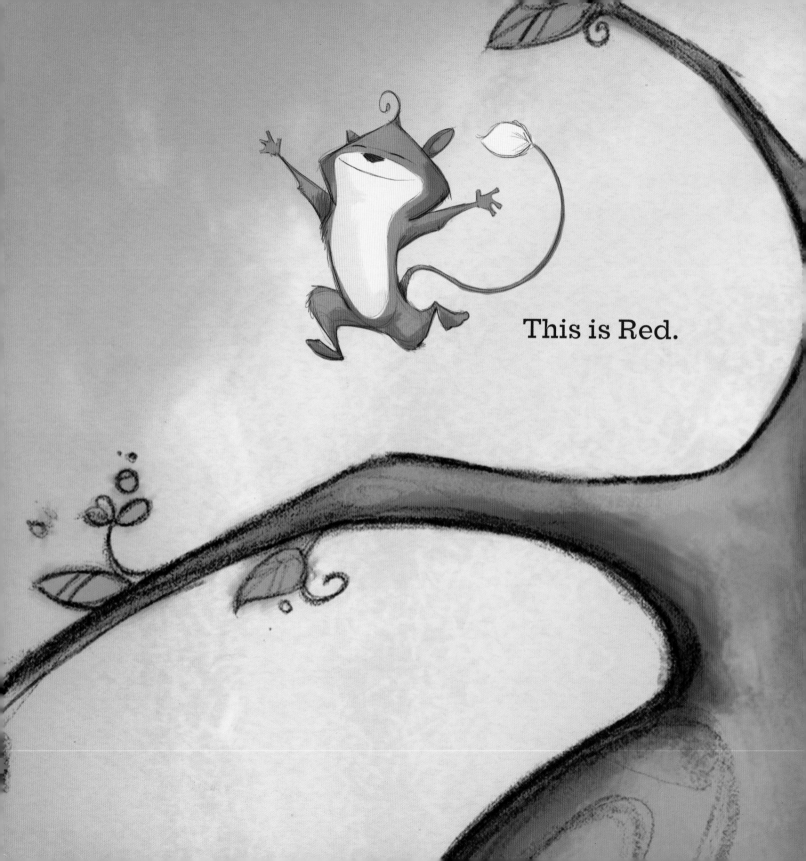

This is Red.

This is Yellow.

They live happily together in
the branches of the Olive Tree.

Some days more happily than others.

One night Yellow was getting
ready for bed when there
was a very loud noise.

It was Red playing
his strummy.

"I'm sleeping,"
Yellow said to Red.

"You don't look like
you're sleeping,"
Red said to Yellow.

"Well, I'd like to be sleeping," Yellow said to Red.

"Oh," said Red.

And Red went back to playing his strummy more loudly than before.

Yellow was upset.

"Stop playing your strummy
so I can sleep!" said Yellow.

Red was also upset.

"Stop trying to sleep so
I can play my strummy!"
said Red.

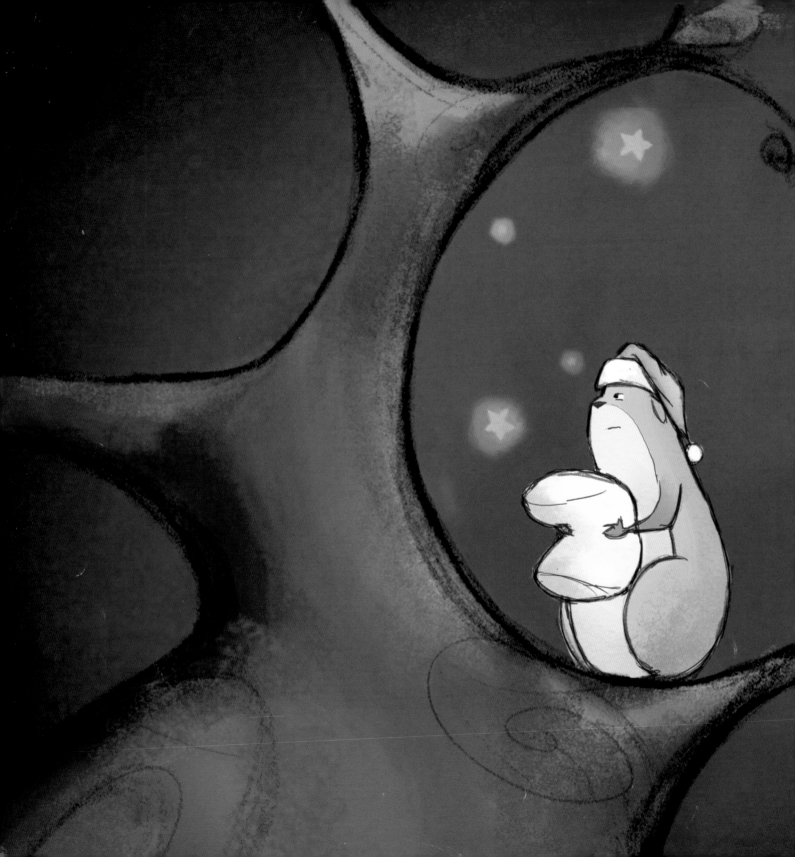

They weren't getting anywhere.

Then Red listened and he heard
that the night was very quiet.

Red began playing
a quieter tune on
his strummy.

Yellow liked it.

Red liked it too.

Then they both had a wonderful idea,
which happens sometimes.

Red played his strummy very
sweetly for Yellow. The sounds of
Red's strummy helped Yellow

fall

asleep.

And everything was good
in the Olive Tree once again.

The End.

# Little Light Foundation

Little Light Foundation is a
non-profit public charity whose goal
is to create original media that helps
children around the world learn about
conflict resolution and mutual respect.
For more information, visit us at
www.littlelightfoundation.org.

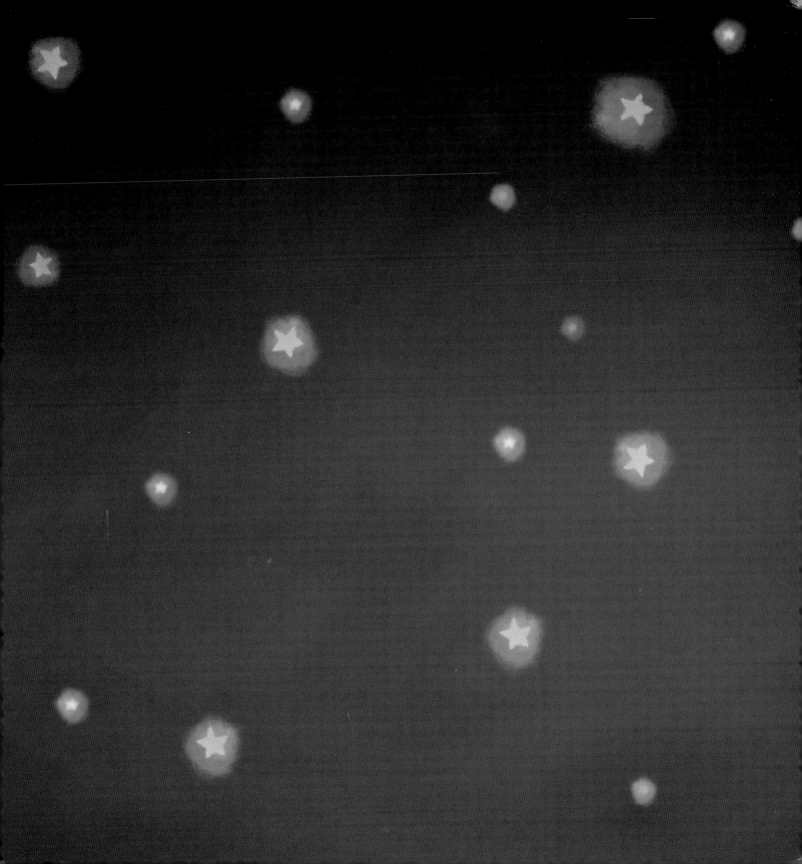